Christmas

Seconds

Cyberworld Publishing

www.cyberworldpublishing.com

ISBN 978-1-921879-52-4

Cyberworld Publishing
Jindalee St
Toronto, Australia

Books By Olivia Stowe

Charlotte Diamond Mysteries

By the Howling

Retired With Prejudice

Coast to Coast

An Inconvenient Death

Savannah Series

Chatham Square

Savannah Time

Other books

Fiddler's Rest

Spirit of Christmas

Christmas Seconds

Christmas

Seconds

A Collection of Inspirational Stories

for the Season

by

Olivia Stowe

Table of Contents

Introduction

The Christmas season is one of seconds: searching for just another second to be able to get everything prepared, second helpings at the holiday table, second thoughts about what it all means and about relationships, and second chances to fulfill the meaningful in gift giving and relationships. *Christmas Seconds* offers up a five-story inspirational novella followed by five separate short stories that also explore the theme of "seconds." The stories in the last section are ones that I have included in what I call my "Christmas Card Tales," because they are very short stories, designed to be included with the cards I send out to celebrate the spirit of Christmas.

The novella titled *Christmas Seconds* is of unexpected opportunities and second chances—and snowballing effects—as a young couple that has been blessed with health and security—and each other—is preparing to embark on a long-delayed honeymoon cruise at Christmas time. As they prepare, they and those they are encountering around them, discover that the true meaning and gift of the season is right there at home—and is in giving of yourself.

In the last section, the short story "Second Helping" is one of hearing the message and quietly responding. "Second Glance" is one of not looking in the right place for the spirit of Christmas—and thus possibly overlooking a treasure. "Second Christmas" stresses that the one getting the most presents isn't necessarily the happiest one, and, similarly, "Seconds" shows that heartfelt gifts may not be the showiest versions. The concluding story, "Second Job," is a celebration of appreciation in the true Christmas spirit.

Christmas Seconds - novella

Second Honeymoon

"I vote for a scarlet one with see-through lace," Cliff whispered in Susan's ear.

"So, no more than eight months' married and suddenly I'm the scarlet woman, am I?" Susan said in her Miss Prim voice. With that, she rolled away from Cliff and off the couch and stood there, hands on hips, giving him her over-the-top pouty look and keeping just out of his reach.

"It was your idea to do a second honeymoon inside a year, toots," Cliff shot back. "That's you playing the fast woman. It's hardly my fault that I see a fast woman as wearing peek-a-boo red."

"Well, we shall see what we shall see. I'm off to Victoria's Secret, and, if you remembered, today's the day you were to sign up for the Bermuda cruise at AAA. So, we'd both best be off."

"Ah, and I'd just gotten the couch warm," Cliff answered. It was now his turn to try out the pouty look and his little-boy-hurt voice.

But Susan wasn't having any of that. She was already half way to the door and grabbing her coat off the back of the wing chair.

"And I want a junior suite with a balcony," she tossed over her shoulder. "I don't care if it will be too cold to sit out there; those are the lowest-price rooms with full-glass walls. I want to see whatever there is to see while we're traveling. I want to know that we are floating on the ocean."

"Money grabber. Tramp. Exhibitionist. Elitist," Cliff tossed out at her. But she was already through the door and revving up her Miata convertible.

Cliff made a note to call AAA from the office. He planned to go in for a few hours today, while everyone else was off for the weekend. It was the only way he could get out in front of the work without all of the distractions of a normal day at the office.

The Claytons were only planning this honeymoon because they'd been married on a national holiday weekend and both had to get back to work the following Tuesday. They'd triangulated between Susan's home town, where they'd tied the knot, and Washington, D.C., where they both had to be at work bright and early two days hence. This process had resulted in two nights at the Foodergong Lodge in Bird-in-Hand, Pennsylvania, for their first, abbreviated honeymoon. Susan had thought the room with the Jacuzzi shaped like a transparent champagne glass was a little too corny, and what was to be their first sanctioned romp in the hay went terribly downhill from there when she had gotten her foot stuck in the stem of the glass à la drain. They'd had to call in the house plumber, he of the sucking teeth and roving eye, to extract her— a little too slowly and too hands on for Susan's taste.

Christmas was the first time they could get free for two weeks, so Susan had insisted that they go for a *real* honeymoon so that she could wipe out the memory of the first try. Cliff had agreed, but only with the stipulation that they considered it their second honeymoon, because he hadn't been at all disappointed with their first one considering what had transpired after the plumber had pulled Susan out of the champagne glass drain and had been convinced to reduce the number of blushing people in the room by one.

* * * *

Susan smiled as she maneuvered the Miata into a tight space near the entrance into Macy's. She did so not just because she had jockeyed for position to get the space with a bottle blonde in a big-ass Mercedes—and lost—only for the blonde to discover that her car didn't fit in the space and Susan's car would. Susan smiled also at the thought of that first honeymoon. She didn't want to forget it at all—and especially the part about that cliché heart-shaped bed—but she certainly didn't mind the chance at a real honeymoon this soon after they'd been married. They deserved this time away together. They both worked hard at their jobs. And they weren't exactly making money hand over fist, although, granted, they were lucky that both were still employed in this economic atmosphere. No, they weren't rich and had been forced to scrimp and save to get what they needed for this trip, short as it was. But still, they were better off than most.

Susan climbed out of the Miata, still thinking of that first night at the Foodergong Lodge. No, she couldn't see that she missed not having to display herself for that plumber more than once. The thought of how ridiculous it all was made her laugh, as she closed the door to walk into the mall. Certainly something to tell the grandkids.

As she gave that little laugh, Susan heard a snort and looked up to see that the blonde of the big-ass Mercedes had apparently found a parking space nearby and was just passing behind the Miata. She was staring daggers at Susan. Then she flipped her head—without moving a single curl of her set-in-cement hair—and flounced off toward the Macy's entrance.

Susan momentarily felt deflated, realizing that the woman had misconstrued her laugh as somehow directed at her. But then Susan decided not to give it another thought. "And a merry, merry, jolly to you, too, sweetheart," Susan mused. Some people just never would get into the Christmas spirit.

Susan was picking out a red, lacey nightie in Victoria's Secret, deciding that if that's how Cliff wanted her, that was how Cliff would get her, when she heard the snort again. It must be her lucky day. Helmet Head Blonde was passing by her again—and giving her that knowing smile of victory. Susan wondered why, until she looked up and saw that she had been pawing around on a "last chance" sales table.

This wouldn't do.

Quite deliberately, Susan dropped the perfectly fine nightie she had found in the pile and turned and surveyed the store. She focused on a rack of obviously best-quality lingerie and made a beeline for it. The nightie she zeroed in on actually wasn't quite as nice, she thought, as the one on the sales table—at least it wouldn't be as flattering to her as that other one would be. But Blondie was still in the store and keeping track of Susan's movements.

"Such a gorgeous nightgown," the sales lady gushed. "I know your man will just drool to see you in it. But, you know, I hope, that you can return it if you decide it's not suitable."

"Oh, that's all right," Susan said in a voice that was a bit too loud if she were only speaking to the saleswoman. But, of course, she wasn't. She was trying to project over to the bra table, where Helmut Head was pretending to look for the biggest cup size on offer. "My husband is taking me on a cruise to Bermuda for Christmas, and I'm sure this will be just perfect."

A half hour later, as Susan was shopping at the lower-end grocery store for the cereal Cliff liked and she could only find here, she was feeling a little testy—with herself. She didn't know why at first, wondering why she suddenly felt out of sorts. But then she thought back on her little challenge match with the Mercedes woman and felt a tad ashamed of herself. It had been so petty and she'd wound up with a nightie that was half as satisfying for twice the price. All because she had let a woman irritate her who had some justification, no matter how mistaken it was, to have been irritated with Susan. On top of that, Susan had criticized the woman's lack of Christmas spirit.

As she moved down the aisle, Susan noticed another woman pushing a squeaky cart ahead of her. She had one toddler boy sitting in the cart and a somewhat older girl hanging onto her skirt. She had a list in one hand, a fist full of store coupons in the other, and a hang-dog look of near collapse of her

18

shoulders that gave Susan the impression she was bearing the cares of the world.

Susan would have zipped around her and grabbed Cliff's cereal and high-tailed it out of a store that she didn't want any of her friends to know she stepped foot in, except that the store was crowded. This store was where many of the people came to who held down more than one substandard job through the week and were forced to shop on Saturday afternoon. There were just too many carts coming at her down the aisle on the other side for Susan to get around the woman pushing the cart so lethargically.

But then, after a few minutes, Susan became mesmerized by the woman and her little girl and toddler son, and she found herself forgetting all about Cliff's cereal and following along behind this young family. The woman was methodical in her shopping, especially considering how little she had in her cart. She would stop and study the shelf, check her list and her coupons, take a can of something really basic—tomato soup or spaghetti in sauce—off the shelf, seem to almost pray over it, and then, more often than not, reluctantly and ever-so-carefully replace it on the shelf. The toddler was snuffling quietly, almost listlessly. In contrast, the little girl was chattering away, asking if they could get this or that—until, at last in the cereal aisle, where Susan had the presence of mind to realize that she had reached her own goal—Cliff's special maple crunch cereal—the little girl pointed at a chock-full-of-sugar cereal that was being pushed hard at American children this month by Kellogg's. She begged her mother to buy a box, and she received a sharp retort in a very tired voice. Susan looked up sharply as the little girl, full of rebellion, if only for a moment, reached out and snatched a box off the shelf and pushed it up and over the top of the side of the cart and into the basket.

The mother stopped dead in her tracks, looked down at the little girl and admonished her in a whisper that Susan couldn't quite hear. The woman hesitated and then, with a sigh that reached Susan's ears, shuffled around in the coupons in her hand as if some cosmic miracle would have put a 100 percent off coupon for that particular cereal in the collection without the mother having noticed it. Coming up blank, the woman reached down and picked the cereal box up and, moving slowly, as if fighting with herself on just what to do, managed to put it back on the shelf. Susan could see tears in the woman's eyes, and then snuffling started in harmony—not just the toddler now, but the little girl also, as the wheels on the woman's cart started to squeak again slowly along the aisle.

This time Susan did not take up her position in the parade. Indeed, why should she? She had reached her goal. She was standing in front of a whole row of Cliff's favorite maple crunch cereal. Beyond this, Susan felt welded to the spot. She had no control over her legs, even though they were trembling slightly. She was plastered to the spot, finding that her eyes were moving between Cliff's cereal and the sugary puffs the little girl had wanted. And she didn't know why, but there were tears in her eyes.

* * * *

Cliff had counted on being alone in the office that Saturday afternoon. He most certainly hadn't counted on trying to think over the sound of a vacuum cleaner out in the hall.

And now the door to his office was opening and howling Hoover sounds were reverberating off his walls.

"Oh, sorry, Mr. Clayton. I didn't think anyone was here today. I'll just take my business over to the other side of the offices. I hope I won't be too noisy over there for you."

"No bother, Clarice," Cliff answered. "There's more reason for you to be here working today than me. Although it's too bad you have to work today. Doesn't your son, Maurice, have his football games on Saturday afternoons?"

"Yes, thas' right, Mr. C. But Saturday is 'big' day for us cleaners. Thas' not only the day when we can do sweeping like this without disturbing folks—beggin' your pardon again, though, for not knowin' you were here. But we also get paid more on a Saturday. More than what we can get for night work even. So I don't turn down no Saturday work here. Not me."

"And you don't mind missing Maurice's games."

"Course' I mind missing them. But my sister, Chanel, takes him mostly and roots for him in my place. She's got a disability; she can't work like I can."

Clarice turned the Hoover and started pushing it back out of the office.

"Well a Merry Christmas to you and your family then, Clarice. I guess you won't have to work that Saturday, Christmas day, at least. I guess you'll have the family all together around a Christmas tree and a big meal with all the trimmings. I've heard what a good cook you are. You do that cake baking over at Hot Cakes, I hear."

"Oh, I don' do that no more, Mr. C. They had to cut back because of the economy and all, ya know. No, it's just this job now. And I'll work that Christmas Saturday if I can. It would mean double time."

"Oh that's a shame," Cliff said. "Having to leave Maurice and your other little guys at home alone with the tree on Christmas day."

"No tree this year, either. Not for our family. I just feel lucky I have this job and we'll still be able to have a roof over our heads and a bit of heat in the grate. No, the way things are down where I live, we'll be living high on the hog this Christmas just to have some boiled ham for sandwiches come Christmas night when I can get home.

"But that's enough jawin' from me, Mr. C. You've come in to get some work done and I'm standin' here just a jawin' and not getting my own work any closer to done. Ya all have a great Christmas yourselves, Mr. C. I'll just go on over to the other side and put this machine on low."

And then Clarice was gone, shutting Cliff's office door behind her with a decisive click.

Cliff had felt pretty good when he'd come into the office. Now, for some reason, he didn't feel pretty good at all. He looked down on the surface of his desk, meaning to get right back into crunching those sales numbers and shaking off this sudden feeling of melancholy. But it wasn't the ledger sheets that caught his eye. It was that note with the number of AAA on it. He'd meant to call AAA and book the cruise to Bermuda as soon as he'd arrived at the office. But he'd forgotten to do so. He reached for the phone.

* * * *

Susan had noticed that Cliff was very quiet and a little withdrawn ever since he had come back from the office. She would have said something—asked him if anything was wrong— but she felt a little nervous and sheepish herself. She needed to talk to him. But she could hardly find a convenient way to slip what she had to say into a conversation with him if he was being unusually reticent and they weren't having a conversation. It was very strange. Cliff wasn't normally like this. He was usually all over her—and joking and making her feel so good about everything. And she did feel good; but she also felt worried. She had no idea how he'd react to what she had to tell him. She opened a beer—and than another. She didn't often drink beer herself, but this was one of those occasions where it might be just what she needed to do. Then she straightened her shoulders and her resolve and marched into the living room and over to where Cliff sat in his armchair, atypically lost in thought.

"Honey, I need to—" she blurted out.

"Susan, I've got to tell you—" Cliff was saying at the same time. Then he flashed a wan little smile and said, "Ladies first."

Susan handed Cliff one of the beers, cleared her throat and wetted her own whistle from the other beer, and sat down on the couch. This was probably not going to be a short conversation.

"I went shopping at the mall for that Scarlet Lady nightie today," Susan said. But then she stopped.

"Ye-s-s-s, and . . . ?" Cliff prompted her after a moment.

"Annnd," she picked up again. "I didn't find anything I wanted. I mean I found something at Victoria's Secret, but after I left the store, I decided it wasn't what I wanted at all. That I would have just felt foolish wearing that for you. So, I took it back. You've always liked the black Teddy. I think I'd like to just go with that one . . . I mean . . . if—"

"No problem with me," Cliff said with a laugh. "You wouldn't be in a nightie for very long, if it was up to me anyway." Then he laughed again, a little nervously this time. "Susan—"

"And I also accepted a dinner invitation for Friday night after next—Christmas Eve," Susan rushed on. "I know it was an impulsive thing to do. But I met this woman and her two kids— a little girl and a darling baby boy—in the Food Lion while I was getting the maple crunch cereal you like so much . . . and we just hit it off . . . and we were buying all of this food . . . and, well, she was so grateful that she asked us over for dinner to share their Christmas Eve dinner. Now I know it sounds strange—"

"Grateful?" Cliff asked. There was a twinkle in his eyes. He hadn't been raised by dummies. He thought he'd caught onto what was going on. And he didn't mind. He didn't mind at all. In fact, it made what he had to say a little easier.

"Yes . . . well, it's sort of complicated. You see—"

"Oh, no need to explain, Susan. I think I know. And this is the Susan I knew I wanted to marry. There's just one glitch, but I think we can work it out."

"A Glitch?" Susan asked. Relieved and suddenly all aglow that she hadn't misjudged the man she had chosen to marry. That they wouldn't be having a row over this.

"Yes, while I was at the office, the cleaning lady, Clarice, was there—I think you remember her, don't you? And we were talking about Christmases and . . . oh, but first, I have a bit of bad news. I couldn't get cruise reservations to Bermuda. They said they were all booked for the sailing that fits with our vacations. So, we'll have to do that another time. I hope you don't mind too much." Cliff rushed on, being a little worried about how Susan would take that vacation-shattering news. But, to his surprise, Susan was giving him a broad smile touched with that "you-sexy-man" look she often gave him just before they headed for the bedroom.

"Anyway," Cliff went on. "Clarice saw that I was a little down at not getting the cruise we wanted, so, out of the blue she upped and invited us over to her place for Christmas Eve to help trim their tree with her family. She's taking her son, Maurice, to a Redskins game that afternoon, but she thought we could come over later. And it might work that we could go to your friends' place for dinner and then desert at Clarice's around their tree. You know Clarice makes a mean cake . . . What? Why are you looking at me like that?"

"Christmas Eve with friends and then Christmas here, just the two of us. It sounds just about perfect to me," Susan said in a hoarse voice that she could barely control. She didn't know when she'd been happier and had felt so good. And she had no idea why she was on the edge of tears. She'd seen the credit card slips on his dresser after he'd come home. She'd wondered what he was doing shopping at that Christmas trimmings store and buying tickets to a Redskins game for while they were supposed to be on a cruise. She figured he'd explain that to her sooner or later. But now he didn't have to.

"But the second honeymoon. I'm sor—"

"Shush, Babe," Susan whispered. She leaned over and gave Cliff a big, sloppy kiss. "We don't have to wait for Christmas for a second honeymoon. And we don't have to go anywhere special for it. Here, stand up and come with me—I'll show you a second honeymoon you'll never forget—starting right now."

Second Sister

"No, I couldn't possibly, Janice. You're wonderful for offering. But, no, of course I couldn't."

"Of course you can, Ann," Janice shot back as she decisively slapped her leather gloves down on the hall table and began to unbutton her coat. "There's no reason at all you can't. And I insist that you stay at the mall for at least five hours. I don't want to see your face back here until four o'clock at the earliest."

"My hair. Just look at my hair, Janice. I haven't been to the hairdressers in I don't know how long. I can't possibly go out looking like this."

"Here, put this on," Janice said, as she darted into the darkened living room and came back with one of Ellen's wigs—

a blonde one, all puffy and starched up like it was a regular on the *Lawrence Welk Show*. "Ugh, where did they find this?" Janice muttered to herself.

"What? What did you say?" Ann asked.

"I said that champagne blonde becomes you. Just look at that." Both women were standing, looking into the mirror over the hall table. Ann looked like a deer just before being introduced to a Mac truck and Janice doing all she could to keep her smiley face intact. To Janice, Ann looked like she'd aged ten years in just these past three months—and Janice wondered with a pang of self-reproach if she hadn't come too late. If Ann hadn't been snappish when they met at the grocery store the other day, Janice wouldn't have even realized that she'd already reached this stage.

Ann was pulling at wisps of hair in the blonde helmet wig, which all just snapped back in place when she let loose of them. "Well . . . But no, I couldn't possibly. I don't even have a car. The Corolla is in the shop. I'm grounded."

"No problem," Janice countered. She had moved over to the closet and was trying to eyeball which coat would be Ann's and which one Ellen's. "You can take my car. I'm not going anywhere. I'm staying here with Ellen while you're gone."

"Oh, I couldn't possibly let you do that . . . ummm, it's the camel hair one to the left there . . . the way Ellen is, I'm the only one . . . no one else should—"

"Ann, honey, you forget that I've already been through this with Cal," Janice said, putting as much determination in her voice as she could muster. She hadn't been sure whether Ann really was open to this, down deep, but Ann—at least subconsciously—had told her which coat was hers. Therefore she mentally was already half way out of the door. So, Janice had no qualms now that this was exactly what Ann needed. "I took care of Cal for nearly a year, and this sort of font of experience isn't something one forgets—ever. You run along now. Here are the keys to the Merc. We'll be just fine."

Ann had been virtually propelled out of her own house. She had no idea why Janice was being such a Christmas angel. The last time Ann had seen Janice—at the grocery store last week—she'd been downright nasty to Janice. But, yet, here was Janice, forcing Ann out of the house and away from Ellen.

Ann knew she was at the breaking point. Obviously Janice had seen that as well and was extra sensitive to it. Janice had finally lost Cal to it in the spring. So Ann guessed she could see when someone in the same circumstance was at the breaking point. Regardless, she was a Christmas angel for actually doing something about it.

Ann loved her younger sister, Ellen, dearly, but theirs hadn't been what you would call a demonstrative family. Ellen was a good seven years younger than Ann and had been born prematurely and always had been a bit on the sickly side. Their miracle baby—that's what their parents had called Ellen. And from the time Ellen had been born, Ann had felt she was leading the life of the "other" child. The one who could always be counted on to behave and to help out. The strong one. The one who didn't need quite so much attention and affection.

And now, now that Ellen had come to live with Ann to be near the hospital for her chemotherapy, Ann couldn't help but feel trapped and put upon. She knew she shouldn't resent it; she loved her sister even though she never felt that Ellen loved her back. That's what Ann firmly believed—that one was required to love their immediate family members. And Ellen hadn't asked for all of the attention Ann was giving her. It was just Ann's way of responding to these situations. It was the way she was raised. Still, she had needs too.

Ann wasn't paying full attention when she pulled into the busy mall parking lot outside the entrance to Macy's. She had been struggling with her feelings again—trying not to feel sorry for herself—and oh so tired—but not winning that battle. If she hadn't been so preoccupied, she would have realized that she couldn't fit Janice's big Mercedes in the spot she was trying to maneuver into. She wasn't driving her Corolla. She swung back out, barely missing a little convertible that had also been angling for that spot.

"Well, I can't fit into the slot," Ann muttered to herself. "That young woman can, though. Good for her."

Ann had found a bigger spot not far away that an SUV was just pulling out of. As she walked down the line of parked cars toward the mall, she passed behind the convertible that had gotten the spot she first tried to fit into just as a young woman was unfolding herself from the vehicle and turning around.

Ann did a double take and emitted an exclamation that came out as something more like a snort. The young woman exiting the small car was the spitting image of her sister Ellen— or at least of the Ellen of two years ago who had been vibrant and elegant and all the other things that Ann had wished to be— but had not been.

Ann was aware that she was staring and not showing the nicest face at this shocking reminder of her sister at a time when they were quite definitely not getting along well, and Ann looked away abruptly, squared her shoulders, and quickened her pace toward the mall.

She was terrible. She really had to put this resentment between her and her sister behind her. True that Ellen had always had and been all of the things that Ann wanted to have and be. But Ellen now had the one thing that changed all of the rest. Ellen had cancer—in an advanced stage. Ellen was facing death, and Ann had the precious thing that Ellen could not count on—good health. If only they had known this two years ago. If only Ellen had known it. Ann had done what she could to be a "best sister"—and Ellen had kept putting her off. Ellen had always seemed to go for the surface pleasures, nothing really meaningful. And Ann had to admit that she'd been openly judgmental about that—probably far too often.

But it was Christmas. Ann always hoped for the best, especially at Christmas time. It had been the one season in her family during which she had been happy—because the spirit of Christmas had always given her hope. No matter what was actually happening in her life.

Ann knew what she'd do. She'd shop for a few Christmas presents for Ellen. Frivolous things, but things with some permanence to them. Nothing to remind Ellen—or herself—how temporary and uncertain life was. Something to make Ellen smile. Ann would give anything to see Ellen smile again—she'd even happily endure the Ellen of two years ago.

Ann decided to start at Victoria's Secret. Ellen had always loved having finely made and sexy lingerie. There was no reason why she shouldn't still have it.

As Ann entered the store, however, she was caught short by an image that transported her in a flash back to two years previously. The young woman from the parking lot—the woman who was the spitting image of Ellen in happier days—was already in the store and was perusing a stack of lacey-red nightgowns. Ann was being confronted with the frivolous self-centered Ellen of such recent times, and all of the resentment and frustration raced back into Ann's mind. She could rationalize her feelings about Ellen and her bad decisions and her lack of appreciation for others away, as she had just been trying to do, but Ann couldn't rationalize away the raw emotions she continued to harbor.

There was a snort and the young woman quickly looked up and her eyes briefly met Ann's again. Ann only half realized that the snort had come from herself and that, once again, she wasn't giving the young woman the best of facial expressions. When she fully realized the effect she was having on the young woman, Ann turned away and moved over to a table where bras were laid out by size. Ann was thinking of Ellen, so she moved to the end of the table with the larger cup sizes. There was no reason why Ellen shouldn't have a nice bra. They had ones here that wouldn't reveal where the scars were.

The young woman moved away from the sales table and Ann saw her move to the more expensive racks in the store. She was picking out what was obviously a very expensive red silk nightgown—just the sort of frivolous expense Ellen would have made two years ago. Ann felt herself praying that the young woman wouldn't buy the nightgown—that she would be moved to reject such expensive play toys while there was still time to make more of her life. That she would realize how fleeting life was and how many needs people other than herself had; that she'd give some thought to what Christmas was all about.

And Ann's heart shrank as she saw the young woman take the red silken nightgown from the rack and carry it over to the sales desk. Ann heard the young woman telling the salesclerk that she was buying it for a Christmas cruise to Bermuda. And Ann was miserable. She turned away and walked out of the store.

She beat herself up in her mind as she stumbled toward the mall's food court, stopping at a coffee café en route for a cup of something hot. She was being crazy and unreasonable to boot. This young woman wasn't Ellen. She hadn't done anything wrong. Ann was just being unreasonable to make this transference. She'd just have to pull herself together and think about something else; this was merely symptomatic of the stress she'd been under in taking such intensive care of Ellen this past couple of months. And she knew, deep down in her heart, that she was only doing that to compensate for her resentment of her younger sister—of her insatiable needs.

But Ann didn't stop thinking of the young woman. Throughout her lunch at the food court and while wandering through the shops picking up this or that which might help cheer Ellen up, Ann found herself praying that something would happen in that young woman's life that would keep her from becoming an Ellen of two years ago—that she wouldn't lose out on life as Ellen had done.

And then, just before the timing of Ann's banishment from her own home was up, Ann's spirits were lifted. She was walking past the entrance of Victoria's Secret, and there was the young woman, back at the counter. All smiles and radiant, as if she'd unlocked some secret to life—and returning that expensive red silk nightgown. Ann had no idea what this meant, other than it made her happy and let her imagine that her prayers had been answered.

Ann didn't park the Mercedes in her driveway when she got home; she parked on the street in front of the neighbor's house. Then she approached the house quietly and from the side, using the back entrance into the laundry room off the kitchen. She was bearing Christmas gifts for Ellen and didn't want to be seen or heard before she was able to tuck them away in the cabinets over the washer and dryer.

When she came into the kitchen, she heard Janice and Ellen conversing in the living room.

Ellen hadn't been downstairs in over two weeks. This was a good sign if Janice had been able to entice Ellen downstairs. Ann had gone to great pains to put up a Christmas tree—using all of the ornaments from their childhood. Trying her best to give Ellen a memorable Christmas for what quite possibly was her last. But Ellen hadn't even come downstairs to see what Ann had done.

Ann would barely make out what her sister and friend were saying, and she found herself drawing quietly toward the door from the kitchen into the dining L off the living room to hear better.

"Then you must tell her so," Janice was saying. "You really must. My Cal told me . . . eventually . . . but it would have meant the world to me if he'd just said those things months earlier."

"I know," Ellen said. "I know I must . . . and sometimes I start to . . . but then I just can't . . ."

"You don't want to make it harder for her? Is that it? Your passing and leaving her behind just when you'd become the greatest of friends? That's what Cal said—that he didn't want me to think of him too fondly, to feel the loss too harshly."

"Yes . . . yes, precisely," Ellen said. "Somehow I think it would be easier for her if she never knew how much I've always looked up to her. How grateful I am she's my sister. How much easier she's made all of this for me."

"You've asked me to help you get a Christmas gift for Ann," Janice said quietly after a long pause. "You know what she'd like best, don't you . . . and I wouldn't even have to go to a store for it, would I?"

"Yes, I guess I know," Ellen said. "I'll try."

"However much time there is left," Janice said, "it will be so much better if you tell her, you know. That's how it was with Cal and me. I know how hard these things are, but—"

"Yes, I'll . . . try," Ellen murmured.

Ann couldn't stay there listening for more. She knew she was about to let loose with a sob that would reveal her presence. She quietly moved back toward the laundry room. She'd go back out to the Mercedes and drive it back up to the house with all of the "I'm arriving" noise she could muster.

She had no idea if Ellen would ever find the courage to tell her how she felt. But that didn't really matter. Now Ann knew already. It made all of the difference in the world. Her Christmas was already complete. And what a true Christmas angel Janice was.

Second Chance

"It would never happen in a million years," Nancy said as she carefully wrapped her apple core inside the plastic wrap from her vanished sandwich. "I mean I'd like to see her better off too—she's a sweet old gal—but Jim Norton signing off on that? Not a chance."

"Well, he's coming this way now; shall we just test it out?" Cliff Clayton retrieved his can of ginger ale from the machine and turned toward the break room door in time to give a nod to Jim Norton, the Norton of Norton and Associates, before looking back at Nancy.

"So, what do you think of that?" Cliff directed the question at Nancy who was sitting at a nearby table, but he had gauged his voice so that he'd be heard by the approaching company CEO.

"About what?" Nancy asked, genuinely confused by this abrupt and confusing change in the conversation.

"About Clarice being snatched from the firm?"

"Oh that," Nancy said, catching on immediately. "The firm would be a disaster without her is what I think." One of Nancy's real attributes for the firm; she was a phenomenally quick study.

"Clarice? Clarice?" Jim Norton couldn't place the name among his employees, but he knew what "snatched from the firm" implied—Sylvester and Sons had just made off with two of his best sales people—and right during the Christmas sales—so Jim Norton was quick to arms at the mere mention of the phrase "snatched from the firm." "What do you mean by that . . . that someone is being snatched from the firm, Cliff?"

"Oh, hi, Jim," Cliff said. "I didn't see you coming in. It's just a rumor, but I've heard that Sylvester and Sons has offered Clarice Walker a full-time job—at twice what we pay her."

"Oh no they don't," Jim Norton snorted as he poured himself a cup of coffee and sat down at one of the tables—not the one that Nancy was at, of course. She wasn't in management. He would have sat at Cliff's table, of course—Cliff was the firm's chief financial officer—but then Cliff was still standing at the drinks machine. Luckily, Cliff wasn't sitting at Nancy's table, or Jim would have had to remain standing.

"We don't want to let this . . . let Clarice go, do we?" This was as much a question as a statement. Jim Norton still didn't have the vaguest notion who the hell Clarice Walker was.

"We certainly do not," Cliff said emphatically. "Why, you know what happened to Singleton's when they let someone as good as Clarice go, don't you? It certainly wasn't a pretty sight. They couldn't find anyone suitable to take that person's place, and the place fell into a shambles. The clients noticed, and they started going elsewhere. And we all saw where that led. No it wasn't a pretty sight. And an employee like Clarice. She really cleans up—and is really organized, always putting the office back in order. Why, any office would kill for the work she does."

Jim Norton still didn't know what Clarice did for the firm, but he was painfully aware that Singleton's had been forced to file for bankruptcy—and right before the Christmas sales season.

"Well, we're not going to lose Clarice, Cliff. Do what you have to do—full staff and triple the salary, if that's what it takes. But just get it done. No more defections from this firm to Sylvester and Sons. Not on my watch."

"I hear you, Jim," Cliff said. "I'll get it done, sir. Don't worry."

Jim Norton moved near Cliff en route to the break room door, full cup of steaming coffee in his hand. Thumping Cliff on the back with the other hand, he said, "Good man, Cliff. Hope you have a great time on that Christmas cruise to Bermuda."

"Oh, Susan and I decided not to go on the cruise, Jim. But thanks. And I'll see what I can do about Clarice right away."

Jim Norton smiled beatifically at his chief financial officer and sailed out the door, having once again averted the disaster of shoals and pirates for the ship he captained. Management was an art; you either had a talent for it or you didn't.

Nancy still sat at the table, her jaw dropped nearly into her lap. "Gee, you're good," she sputtered. "I was positive you couldn't get Jim Norton to do that."

"It's all in the wrist action," Cliff said with a smile.

"But do you think he has any idea that Clarice is the office cleaner?"

"Not a chance," Cliff said. "But I don't regret it a bit. Clarice is, indeed, worth full benefits and three times what we're paying her now. I'm just sorry that, like so many others, I've just been looking through her and taking her for granted all these years."

* * * *

Clarice Walker had to sit down and try to catch her breath. Luckily there was a rush-bottom chair next to the table by the front door, even though it was barely substantial enough to hold Clarice, let alone any of her healthy-appetite sons.

The hand she was holding the letter in was shaking so hard that she had trouble rereading what it said. Ever since she had been cleaning the offices of the Norton company last Saturday and had stumbled on that nice Mr. Clayton working in his office, she had believed there really was a Santa Claus. Mr. Clayton had actually talked with her. She was so used to people just looking through her in her work life—the few who were actually around when she was working—that it had been a shock he'd asked her how she was doing. Then she thought she'd spoiled it all by telling him the truth—how she had lost her second job baking cakes at Hot Cakes; how rough it was working Saturdays when her eldest boy, Maurice, was playing in those football games that a parent should be going to; how they didn't have the wherewithal to even have a Christmas tree this year—and thus why it was just as well that she'd be working the Christmas Day Saturday.

Lord knew she had not been angling for that young Mr. Clayton to play Santa—not in the least—but he had launched right into that role. Before she'd finished cleaning that day, he'd called out and had a trimmed tree and enough holiday food to choke a whole passel of horses sent over to her house—her sister, Chanel, had called her all excited about that—but he also had given her vouchers for three tickets to the Redskins Christmas Eve pro football exhibition game. He said that something should be done for her son Maurice to make up for the inconvenience the firm had laid on them all this time that kept his mother from seeing his games.

That was a real bonanza in itself. But now here was this letter from the Norton firm. Signed by that old scowling Mr. Norton himself—offering her a full-time position with Norton and Associates, with full benefits and all—to be their exclusive cleaning staff. And three times what she had been making with them as a casual vendor as well as time worked to be at her discretion as long as it was outside normal business hours. She could work Saturdays if she wanted—but she could arrange to go to Maurice's football games on Saturdays if that suited her too. Just as long as she got the work done.

Clarice had never had a Christmas like this. No one had given her a second glance before this, let alone all of these truly good things. Not least those Redskins tickets. Clarice's thoughts went back to those tickets.

Miracle that it was, those three tickets put Clarice in a dilemma. She guessed that Mr. Clayton had assumed there was a Mr. Walker in the picture. But there hadn't been a Mr. Walker for a good many years, and there now wasn't even a Leroy, who was the last man Clarice had let into her bed, anywhere around.

Leroy had lost his job in the summer and, after a few weeks of moping around the house, had just walked out on her and the boys. Clarice couldn't say she had gotten over that; she'd thought Leroy was "the one," and the boys seemed to have taken to him real well too.

What to do with that third ticket? Maurice had to go, of course. He was the reason she had the tickets. And she couldn't not go herself. It had been clear that Mr. Clayton gave these tickets to her so that she and Maurice would take in a game together. She certainly couldn't take one of the younger boys and not the other. And although her sister Chanel deserved to go as big a help she'd been with the boys while Clarice tried to hold down two jobs, if the younger boys couldn't go, Chanel would have to stay back and take care of them.

So, Santa had brought Clarice a real problem. A problem most folks would love to have, of course, but Clarice wasn't accustomed to having nice problems. Cleaning up after folks usually brought only the other kinds of problems. She was sort of lost on handling good choices.

Clarice thought long and hard about how to dispense those tickets. She was saved by a knock at the door, however.

She went to the door, and suddenly all of those not-so-nice problems came rushing back in.

"Leroy," she said with a gasp. And suddenly she was flooded with all those fighting emotions—anger and fear and pique and desire and relief that he was still alive.

"Howdy, Clarice," Leroy said. He was holding his baseball cap in his hands, as if it meant something to Clarice that he had taken it off in her presence, and he was staring at the ground, not being able to look at her eyes.

They just stood there, Leroy's eyes concentrating on a loose board on the step up to the porch and Clarice digging hard into the top of his head with her intent gaze.

Leroy cleared his throat. "Nice day, tain't it?"

"Yes, yes it is, considering it's a mite cold for December and drizzling," Clarice responded in as even a tone as she could manage.

"Kind of a day that makes a man thirsty, though," Leroy observed.

"You can come in for a cup of coffee to warm yerself, Leroy. But don't plan on puttin' down any roots."

They were at the kitchen table when Clarice finally calmed down enough to ask him what was burning in her mind. "I see you're still alive and kickin'. So, where'd you go and why'd you suppose that was what you wanted to do?"

"It wasn't what I wanted to do, Clarice. But it's what I thought I had to do at the time. Me without a job and you workin' so hard and supportin' me as well as the boys. Well, I wasn't pullin' my weight here and it was gittin' to me."

"So you left us, without a word," Clarice said.

"Would it have been all right if I'd said I was goin', Clarice? Would you have smiled and waved your hanky and sung toodaloo to me?"

Clarice didn't answer that. She had no idea what she would have done. Begged him to stay? Screamed obscenities at him the whole neighborhood could hear? What she did know, however, was that she was robbed of expressing any opinion on his going at all.

"It was only for a while, Clarice. I went down to Louisiana and helped put up new houses to replace those taken down by the hurricane. Just until I had enough money to keep up my end here—and until I could find another job up here. Which I've done now. I start down at Home Depot next week."

"So you jist up and went off without a word of why or what?" Clarice continued to dig.

"I wrote. I did write. But I sent the letters to Maurice at his friend, Sean's, house. I couldn't write direct. I couldn't stand it if you didn't write back if I wrote direct. It was better if I was writing through Maurice. And you didn't write back. If you had written back in anger, I don't think I'd have had the courage of comin' here today. But maybe that's what you'd have preferred."

"There's a good reason I didn't answer none of them letters," Clarice said. And then she turned her head and called out, "Maurice. Maurice Walker, get your behind in here. Right now."

When Maurice arrived, his eyes got big at the sight of Leroy Jefferson sitting in his mother's kitchen again, and he completely failed to conceal his excitement and relief—and, especially that telltale glimmer of hope that betrayed how he felt toward this man who had taken his dead daddy's place for nearly a year.

The look was not lost on Clarice.

"Maurice, what's this that Leroy tells me about you gettin' letters from him and not passin' anything on to me?"

"I was afraid, I'm sorry, Momma," Maurice mumbled into his chest—he, like Leroy, not being able to maintain eye contact with his mother.

"Afraid? Afraid of what, boy?" Clarice asked sharply.

"Afraid you'd tell me I had to stop gettin' the letters," Maurice muttered. And then in a stronger voice, "And afraid you'd get hurt again, Momma. If Leroy wasn't comin' back, I didn't want you to have the disappointment of the possibility he would. I know how you took it when Daddy died."

Things were so quiet in that kitchen for the next couple of minutes that all three found themselves concentrating on the snoring the youngest, Dansel, was doing in the next room.

"Well. Well," Clarice said eventually. "Look at the two of you. Maurice has a football practice today, and I've got to get off to work. Do you think you can stick around long enough to get him to that, Leroy?"

"Yes, ma'm," Leroy answered, all smiles, and looking up into Clarice's face for the first time since he'd arrived.

"But that's it for now, Leroy Jefferson," Clarice continued. "Don't think you're gettin' your shoes back under my bed this soon. You go find yourself someplace to live—at least for a while—and then we'll see what we have to see."

"Yes, ma'm," Leroy answered.

"And do you have anything goin' already for Christmas Eve?" Clarice asked.

"No, ma'm," Leroy answered.

"That's good. Because we're having people for dinner— a nice young couple from Norton's; I think you'll like them— and I have tickets for Maurice, me—and you, if you're interested—to the Redskins game earlier that afternoon."

"Yes, M'AM," Leroy answered—all smiles, hugging Maurice close to keep both of them from jumping out of their skins for joy.

It didn't escape Clarice that Maurice was hugging Leroy close too. Yes, she thought, trying not to show too broad a smile to her two wayward men, this was certainly shaping up to be a much better Christmas than she had imagined it would be. But

Clarice had learned not to ask too many questions of life; she was more than happy to give life a second chance.

Second Christmas Tree

Viv reached for the phone. It was the first time today that it had been quiet in the house. Both Travis and Katie were down for their naps.

She had intended to call her parents, but the number she instinctively punched in was that of her agent. She knew she shouldn't be bugging Angela, that Angela told her she's learn something just as soon as Angela heard something, but Viv was so, so very close to the end of her endurance, not to mention her savings. The phone rang but no one answered.

Viv's hand was shaking as she put the receiver down, and she had to hold the coffee cup with both hands to get it to her mouth without spilling it down the front of her blouse. Maybe a couple of more swallows and she'd build up the courage she needed to try calling her parents again.

It was almost Christmas. It was crushing that she hadn't talked with her parents since September and that she may not see them during the holidays. Christmas had always been a family time. The lack of contact was mostly her fault, yes, but her mother was so stubborn about this too. She'd never liked Rob and said he'd leave Viv someday. They'd had that big fight over that. And, of course, her mother was right; Rob had walked out on Viv. But that wasn't all. Her parents had never supported Viv in her dream—to be a published novelist. Her mother had told her once, when Viv and Rob had had a crockery-against-the wall fight, that Viv and the kids were always welcome to come home—but only if Viv gave up on her writing and got a job that would help pay the added bills.

Viv couldn't give up her dream; she was her mother's daughter as far as stubbornness went. She thought that writing was the only thing left that gave her life value.

Feeling a little more steady after several gulps of coffee, Viv reached for the telephone again, but Travis picked just that moment to wake up and start fussing—and, of course, his fussing wakened Katie as well.

Viv's hand wavered over the telephone receiver, and then she sighed and stood up and opened the kitchen cupboard. The moment of almost courage was past. The cupboard didn't give her any cheer either. Poetic versions of "but the cupboard was bare" ran through her mind as she realized that after she'd fed the kids some lunch, they'd have to go off to the Food Lion if they were to get any supper. There weren't many more suppers that Viv could eke out of what was left in her bank account. Something was going to have to give soon—within days. She'd have to go hat in hand to her parents and give up on her dream or check out whether she could get any writing done in a homeless shelter.

"Merry Christmas," Viv muttered to herself as she moved toward the bedroom and her real-world responsibilities.

* * * *

At first, Viv thought the young woman was deranged. And that was all she thought she needed now—being accosted by a mad woman by the checkout counter at the downscale grocery store while she was trying to shuffle store coupons and what little cash she had to bring them into the best balance she could while juggling two snuffling children. Today was turning out to be just perfect. Just what she needed to put her into the holiday spirit. Even on second thought, after the woman had introduced herself as Susan Someoneorother and was still just standing there hugging that box of sugar pop cereal, Viv thought she might be deranged.

"I'm sorry," the Susan person final said. "But I thought . . . I wondered . . . Oh, damn, I've never done this before, but I just wondered if there was anything I could do to help."

And then she just stood there, expecting Viv to take the next step, no doubt. Although, no, she didn't just stand there. She pushed the box of sugar pop cereal out at arms' length, and Viv's six-year-old daughter, Katie, snatched it and rewarded the young woman with a squeal of glee.

"I'll pay for it, of course," the young woman blurted out. "I just would like your little girl have it . . . if . . . if it's OK with you, of course. You'd be doing me a great favor. And if I could help you with—"

"Thank you, but . . ." Viv cut in as she started to reach over to take the box of cereal away from Katie. But she stopped with her hand wavering in midair. She couldn't do it. She just couldn't do it. She'd known the woman was following along behind them down the grocery store aisles, and she could understand now that the woman had seen how few items Viv had taken off the shelf and how desperately she'd looked through her fistful of coupons, trying to match them to necessities she could stretch her money to cover. And she knew she had left the woman behind in the cereal aisle when Katie had put up that fuss about wanting a box of the sugar pop cereal and Viv had been forced to put it back on the shelf.

Viv wasn't the one to take charity—or even to acknowledge when she needed it. She had her pride; there wasn't much of anything else left for her to cling too. And of course she couldn't let the woman just give Katie that box of cereal. But Viv was at the end of her rope. She looked into Katie's excited eyes, and she just couldn't take that box of cereal away from Katie again. Even though it was just a box of cereal. But it was a box of cereal she herself couldn't possibly buy.

Viv solved her dilemma by slumping into her cart, practically into the lap of her toddler, Travis, who was sitting in the cart all wide eyed and just fixing to wail in complaint about the present Katie had gotten and he hadn't.

"Here, there are tables over there by the deli counter," Susan was saying as she reached out and held Viv, keeping her from falling into the cart. "Let's just sit over there for a minute and have a cup of coffee and talk for a few minutes. I need to talk with you, but I don't even know what to say."

For the next twenty minutes, Susan proved she didn't know what to say but that she had no trouble talking. She was babbling some sort of nonsense at Viv about needing to help her and the kids with some groceries, even though she understood how hard it was to accept help, but that she needed to do this for herself. That she just couldn't sleep if she didn't know she'd helped. And at first she also was running off about red silk nightgowns and Victoria's Secret and how that was not really her, not what she wanted at Christmas. But when she got over that confusing data dump and Viv had gotten a chance to pull herself together better, Viv started to believe that this Susan person really did want to help her. And then Viv started to just let it all pour out herself—it had been ages since she'd had a girlfriend of her own that she could just let it all out with. How her husband and left her and she was too scared and proud to contact her parents, and how close they were to losing the apartment and not having anything to eat, and how frightened she was that if she told anyone about it they'd take away her kids, and how tantalizing close she thought she was to selling a manuscript and pulling a fairytale ending out of all of this.

"I understand," Susan said at length. "You just need a little bridge going for you here. Please let me help a little. It would mean so much to me."

"I know I'm being selfish and stubborn," Viv said, her voice low and plaintive, as if she was trying to convince herself more than Susan. "But I have this dream of making it as a writer. It's the only thing I have left."

"Are you sure it's the only thing you have left?" Susan asked. She looked across the table at the beaming faces of two small children slurping on the boxed drinks Susan had gotten at the deli counter along with the coffees for Viv and her. Katie was still holding the box of sugar pop cereal close to her breast and, having followed Susan's gaze over at the kids, Viv wondered whether the sugar pops inside the box would be pulverized before they could get them home.

"You have them too," Susan said. "And of course you have to keep them with you. Just let me help a little. Just through Christmas. I'll bet you don't have a tree for them yet, do you?"

"No," Viv said. "I don't have a coupon for one of those." They both laughed at that, Susan a little nervously and Viv a little bitterly. But then they heard the tinkle of happy laughter from Katie and Travis from across the table, happy because the adults were happy and everyone was getting along so well, and then Viv's and Susan's laughs became more loose and natural.

That's when Travis decided he needed a bathroom. Right NOW.

Susan said she'd wait there with Katie if Viv wanted to take Travis to the bathroom, and as Viv stood up, Susan asked, "By the way, you look familiar to me. Maybe we were together in school. What was your name then?"

"Rievers," Viv answered absentmindedly. "Vivian Rievers. I went to Peyton High. You?"

"No, I went to Stanley," Susan answered. "Guess we didn't know each other then."

Viv had left her purse in the flurry of activity in taking Travis off to the bathroom, and Katie didn't seem to notice as

Susan stuck her hand into the purse and fished around for an address book.

When Viv returned, she had come to an acceptance of suspension of her pride, if only through Christmas. Susan was really nice, and she didn't seem half as crazy now as she had at first. Viv was already thinking how this scene would fit into a novel.

Viv agreed to another sweep through the store to triple what she had put in the cart the first time—enough to see the three of them into the New Year—plus a few Christmas season treats for the kids.

When they came out into the parking lot and approached Susan's small two-seater Miata convertible, Susan laughed at the prospect of getting the four of them and all of the groceries into the tiny vehicle. Viv didn't laugh, though. She instantly thought that this was where the dream would end, where reality set in and her brief escape from depression evaporated.

But then Susan reached into her purse and snapped open a cell phone and started punching numbers.

"What—?"

Susan held up a finger. "Hello, can you send a taxi to the Food Lion on 12th and Main? Oh, good . . . and, oh, do you have a van or SUV taxi you can send? That's right . . . Thanks."

"A van?" Viv asked. "Why a—?"

"I'm figuring all of us and these groceries and a Christmas tree won't fit in a regular taxi," Susan said.

Viv was speechless, but Katie's eyes got big and she started clapping her hands. Travis was much too engrossed with a candy cane to care much what the adults were talking about.

While they waited for the taxi, Susan said she had another call to make and, as she moved to the far side of the store façade and paced back and forth while having what obviously was a very serious phone conversation, Viv and Katie watched her anxiously, as if she was an apparition that would call out "December Fool" at any point and just disappear in a puff of smoke. Travis was totally engrossed with the delicious stickiness of his candy.

A couple of hours later, when Susan had helped Viv get a tree that was much too big for the apartment's living room up and trimmed with what Susan had bought at the Christmas store and shortly after Viv had gotten Susan to at least agree to come to a modest Christmas Eve dinner and bring her husband, Susan left all smiles and glowing. Then an overentertained Katie and Travis had voluntarily stomped off for naps that should have come a couple of hours earlier, and Viv was left alone. For the first time all afternoon the merry-go-round had slowed enough for her to take stock of all that had happened. And, as a result, her euphoria started to trickle down the dial again and the doubts began to seep in. She went over to the table by the door and picked up the mail that had come through the slot in the front door while she and the kids had been off on their fairytale buying spree.

She was so lost in thought that she didn't even look at the return addresses on the envelopes as she opened them. So, she didn't notice either that she was opening a letter from her literary agent, Angela, or that a check floated to the floor as she unfolded the letter. She read the letter. And then she read the letter again. This was unlike any of the rejection letters she'd been receiving for months. Then she read the letter again, catching on for the first time that it referenced an advance check from a mainline publishing house for her latest manuscript. She looked around for the check and, not finding it in the envelope, scrabbled around on the floor until she found it. She had to check the number of zeros twice before she would accept what was written there. $20,000. She was holding an advance check for $20,000.

Tears came to Viv's eyes as she rose from the chair and stumbled toward the telephone. She had all the courage she needed now to call her parents.

As Viv moved toward the kitchen, however, the door bell chimed, and she instinctively swerved and looked through the small-paned windows running up beside the door before opening it. She couldn't believe it. Out in the hall, ringing her door bell were . . . both of her parents, her mother's arms full of wrapped Christmas presents and her dad struggling with an impossibly tall and full pine tree.

"What," she thought idiotically while laughing hysterically, "are we going to do with two Christmas trees?" as she fought with hands still clutching an advance check for $20,000 to unlatch the door. What a difference a trip to the grocery store had made.

Second Sight

"But don't you find it just a tad bit strange?" Cliff Clayton asked his wife, Susan. Even though they were sitting knee to knee on rickety kitchen chairs, they barely could see each other through the decorated and lit pine branches. Two bushy Christmas trees, enveloping the room in a strong, eerie light, were positioned in the small living room, in opposite corners, but with their branches almost touching in the center of the room.

"Shh, she'll hear you," Susan muttered back at Cliff out of the side of her mouth.

"And you're saying you—actually we—bought her one of these?"

"Yes," Susan whispered back. "But ours was the first one—and I had no idea how small this room would be or I wouldn't have gotten one so bushy. Once I got started, I just couldn't stop. The Christmas spirit can grab you like that . . . Oh, thanks, Katie. I don't mind if I do."

Susan had suspend the sotto voce conversation with her husband to accept a handful of sugar pop cereal from a bowl a smiling girl of six was holding out to her. The girl then proffered the bowl to Cliff. He leaned out beyond the pine branches and tossed a question mark look at his wife and then, prompted by Susan, took a small handful of the sugar pops and thanked the delighted six-year-old. Katie then turned and skipped off toward the kitchen, very pleased with her hostess abilities. The young woman Susan had befriended and then helped, Viv, was standing in the kitchen with her parents and pouring over a letter and talking with happy, animated gestures. Cliff felt something sticky slide across his forearm and turned toward a high chair that was sitting very close to his knee. A toddler, a boy, was holding out the slick, thinned-to-a-point end of a nearly devoured candy cane and gurgling his offer of a guest suck, mimicking what his sister had done with her precious sugar pops.

After voicing a very sincere "Thanks, but I wouldn't think of taking any of your candy," Cliff turned his head toward Susan, confused and wondering if they should make a bolt for it while the other adults were still occupied with that letter in the kitchen. Cliff and Susan were supposed to be at sea, steaming into Kings Warf, Bermuda, right now and enjoying a black tie captain's dinner of lobster tail and champagne.

"What's with the cereal?" he queried Susan, while he smiled at the toddler and made clear a second time that he had no intention of depriving the boy of even one single lick of that precious candy cane. The offer made twice and appropriately turned down, the boy proved delighted to work on the candy cane all by himself.

"Don't ask," Susan said. And then she laughed. "Although I'll tell you later. It's what brought me together with Viv's family. I still can hardly believe that I was so forward with her—and that I ruined our plans like I did."

"You didn't ruin our plans," Cliff answered. "I was off doing worse to our Bermuda cruise plans myself."

"So, do you regret we gave up our Bermuda cruise second honeymoon to be eating sugar pops as an appetizer for our Christmas Eve dinner?" Susan asked. And her face took on a strained look. She still wasn't sure about what she'd done. She'd seen a young family in the grocery store that obviously was down on its luck and possibly might not get enough to eat through the Christmas season even beyond having a Christmas with tree and everything. And she'd impulsively dropped her own plans to buy expensive lingerie for a second honeymoon cruise and forced her good will on this family. Even more strange, she'd done this without knowing that at the same time Cliff was using the money meant for the cruise to help the cleaning lady, Clarice, at his firm through a tough Christmas season as well. The upshot was that they were having their Christmas Eve dinner here with Viv's family and going on to the cleaner's house for desert.

"No, not sorry in the least," Cliff answered. "We can take the cruise later—at any time. Christmas comes only once a year. And I'm not sure I really was looking forward to that cruise at all." And having said it, Cliff realized that this was true. It was something he hadn't thought about. Now that he had given it a thought, he had to recognize that there was some other motive than a second honeymoon that had made him suggest a cruise this Christmas. He'd have to think about that—when he didn't have to stay on his toes just to keep up with the near insanity of what was happening around him right now. Viv and her parents seemed to have been finished in the kitchen and were emerging with plates of food. For right now Cliff would have to concentrate on how to cut slabs of beef on a plate perched on his lap—and to keep it from being swept away by a swaying pine branch.

"We were just going over the letter from the literary agent again," Viv said as she and her parents entered the room, the women carrying plates of food and her father dragging two more chairs along with little prospect of finding some place in this indoor pine forest to set them down.

"I still can't believe that everything has come together like this," Viv continued. "First you, Susan, with your Good Samaritan attention to me and Katie and Travis—and then this big advance arriving from a publisher and my parents, who I hadn't been in contact with for months, showing up all at the same time. Why, I don't know how such a wonderful Christmas materialized just like that . . . my parents, Susan. They told me. They told me that you called them. I don't know how to thank—"

"Oh, no," Susan interjected. "I should thank you. This has made my best Christmas ever, I think. And with that advance, you paid back whatever I was putting into it right away. I couldn't be any more happy."

"I know I can never do enough," Viv said. "You gave me courage . . . and hope. And my parents. Even without the advance, my life was enriched. And . . . it's not nearly enough . . . I know. But I want you to know that I'm dedicating my next manuscript to you. The novel I'm writing now is about hope."

"I don't know what to say," Susan murmured, the light from the overpowering trees gleaming in the tears forming in her eyes.

Cliff knew what to say, but he knew this wasn't the time or place to say it. The lights on the trees were affecting him too.

His thought at the moment was that he was awfully glad that Viv had also gotten that $20,000 advance for her book, because he didn't want to be around and on the hook for the electricity bill being generated by the lights on these two gigantic Christmas trees.

Later in the evening Susan and Cliff regrouped on the front porch of Clarice Walker's narrow wooden house in a neighborhood both normally avoided. Cliff had come from the office and Susan from home, so they were driving in separate cars.

Susan was a little apprehensive about meeting Clarice, the cleaner at Cliff's firm, Norton and Associates. But from the moment Clarice met them at the door, one of her gourmet coconut cakes with crème filling in one hand, both Susan and Cliff were lost in her nurturing hospitality.

She and her eldest son, Maurice, and what appeared to be Clarice's boyfriend, Leroy, had just returned from a first-time-ever Redskins exhibition football game, where the Redskins had trounced Dallas, and the exuberance in this house couldn't have possibly been higher. Cliff had bought them the tickets as part of his effort to lift Clarice's spirits to the level of the Christmas session—and had done so with a large chunk of the cash that originally had been put aside for the second honeymoon cruise to Bermuda. But it was only now that Cliff realized it had been fortuitous that he had bought three tickets. He had intended for

Clarice and Maurice to go to the game—to make up for all of Maurice's Saturday football games Clarice had missed because she had to be cleaning the Norton firm offices then—but Cliff had never intended for there to be a third ticket. It had been a slip of his finger when he was ordering tickets from the Internet that he had bought three rather than two tickets. Now, however, he could see that this had been prescient—almost as if he'd had second sight. He'd had no idea that there was a Leroy in Clarice and Maurice's scene, but he could see in how exuberant all three of them were in the experience they had shared that this had been a significant event—for all three of them combined—in their lives.

For some reason, as they were eating desert, and all talking at once, animated and happy as could be, Cliff was struck with something having occurred in what he had done for Clarice that was far greater in effect than just in what he had put into it. It had been expensive for him and Susan, yes, and it had pushed their own plans aside, but something larger than everyone assembled had happened here—and Cliff understand, without fully knowing why, that this had been more of a bonding experience for him and Susan than a second honeymoon in Bermuda and a red-lacy nightie for Susan could ever have been.

It was at that point that both Cliff's and Susan's cell phones chimed, almost simultaneously, and both were expelled out of the convivial, comfortable atmosphere of the Walker home, both in panic and consternation.

Susan was launched toward the hospital west of town. Her younger sister, Sissy, was having her baby. This wasn't supposed to happen for three weeks yet. Susan and Cliff were supposed to be safely home from Bermuda before Sissy gave birth. But it was happening now, and Susan's tearful mother was saying that it was touch and go and that Sissy was in a panic.

As Susan raced across town, it struck her that if she'd been on the Bermuda cruise now, she wouldn't be here for the premature birth and all of the dangers that entailed. And then it struck her, even harder, that it was her sister's impending delivery of a child that had made the Bermuda cruise so attractive to Susan. She had resented her sister having a baby. For the first time Susan accepted that this was so. Susan wanted a baby and hadn't gotten pregnant yet. Sissy wasn't even married—and was younger than Susan—and she was having a baby. And the whole family had been swept up in Sissy having a baby and needing their support. Susan had felt left out. So, Susan had jumped at the suggestion that she and Cliff take off for Bermuda for Christmas. And Susan had decided she needed to go out and buy herself sexy red lingerie.

"How classic," Susan muttered as she raced for the hospital. Jealousy and screaming for attention. All because she was jealous. And she'd only been saved by some force—inside her or acting on her—to think of someone other than herself in this Christmas season. Something inside her had seen what she hadn't seen and had compelled her to change her plans. And now her little sister was in the hospital—in danger—and having a first baby much too early. Susan rubbed the blinding tears from her eyes and whipped into the hospital parking lot.

* * * *

Meanwhile, headed toward a hospital connected to a nursing home on the opposite end of the town, Cliff was racing at an equally swift pace. The night supervisor of the nursing home had called him to tell him that his father was failing fast and that he would need to come right away just in case his dad didn't make it through the night.

How could this be? Cliff, thought, as he ran out of Clarice's and to his car. He'd seen his father just a while ago and he'd seemed fine. It was only when Cliff was alone in the car— alone with his thoughts and turning his driving instincts over to maneuvering the familiar roads and turns out to the nursing home, a trip he'd made a couple of times a week for over a year, that Cliff admitted that he had been fooling himself. He knew his dad was failing. He had blocked it out—especially because it was happening at this time of year. His father had been a Christmas Day baby, so Christmas had always meant something extra special around their house when Cliff had been growing up. And Christmas had revolved around his dad.

Cliff was walking into the entrance of the nursing home when the full ramifications of his self-denial hit him, and he had to sit down on a sofa in the lobby for several minutes to reason through what was racing through his mind and get control of himself before he went to his father's room. Not only had he been into denial about his father's failing health, but he also had rebelled at listening to his father when he had tried to discuss his impending passing with Cliff—and Cliff had gone to the lengths of planning the cruise to Bermuda for now. Not really because he and Susan just had to go on a second honeymoon right at this time—but more to flaunt the denial that Christmas was in any way a danger period for his father. Cliff was intellectually aware—just not emotionally accepting—that Christmas was a time when people in failing health often died—that they held on just to get to Christmas and then, having met—or almost met, if they just couldn't hang on long enough—that goal, they just gave up the effort and expired. And, with his father, it wasn't just because of Christmas. This also would be his dad's seventy-sixth birthday.

And, in total denial, Cliff had planned a Christmas cruise to Bermuda. His father must think he was in Bermuda now, in fact. He'd forgotten to tell him that he and Susan had changed their minds.

When Cliff reached his dad's room, which was in semidarkness, lit only by the white lights on a miniature Christmas tree on the dresser at the foot of his father's bed, under the now-blacked-out TV set attached to a shelf high on the wall above it, Cliff immediately tuned into his father's breathing. It was ragged and belabored and shallow—the sort of breathing where those listening to it suspended their own breath in the pauses and wondered, with a clutchy feeling, whether there would be another breath. A nurse was sitting beside his father's bed. She had been holding his hand, and Cliff had the wrenching feeling of self-reproach that someone other than he was doing that—followed by a flood of appreciation that the nurse was there. She looked up at Cliff with that expression of sadness-laced inevitability that everyone fears seeing and silently rose and, after laying a hand on Cliff's shoulder briefly, slipped by him and out into the brightly lit corridor. Cliff murmured his thanks as she passed, and her eyes lifted to his in an expression of sympathy and surprise—revealing how rarely the relatives of her charges realized she even was there. As she walked into the light of the corridor, there was an aura around her that made Cliff think of halos. And Cliff thought that fitting, that nurses like them deserved halos.

Cliff sat on the seat the nurse had vacated, a seat warmed by her presence for who knew how long, and he took up his father's hand.

"Hi, Dad, it's me, Cliff?"

"Cliff? Cliff? I thought you were in Bermuda."

"No, Dad, We decided to stay home for Christmas. We are coming to see you tomorrow, Dad. Your birthday. We wouldn't miss that." A truth and a lie. When their plans changed, Susan and he did, indeed, plan to spend part of Christmas Day with his dad. But a lie in the claim that Cliff would not have missed being here for Christmas. He had planned, in his attempt to escape an unwanted realty, not to be here. It was just some force outside of himself—that chance locking into the problems of the firm's cleaning lady, that had intervened. Some insight that something inside himself had perhaps.

"Yes, my birthday," Cliff's dad mumbled. "Wouldn't want to miss that."

"No, we wouldn't, would we?" Cliff said. "And I'm sorry. We have a gift; I forgot to bring it tonight. Tomorrow, for sure."

"A gift?" his dad said. There was a long pause, and then, with great effort, Cliff's dad spoke again. "You know what would be the best gift, Cliff?"

"No, Dad, what would be the best gift?"

"I think most of all . . . I would like to see your mother again and visit with her. I look forward to that."

Then Cliff knew his dad truly was ready. Cliff's mother had passed on three years earlier. Cliff started to speak, but a lump in his throat prevented that for several minutes. He knew what he needed to say, though. He didn't want to say it. But say it he must. And when at last he felt he could get the words out, he did so.

"It's OK, Dad, I understand. We'll be fine. It's OK."

Just then the hour struck in the big grandfather's clock just down the corridor in the family visitation area, and Christmas Eve turned into Christmas Day.

"Merry Christmas, son," Cliff's dad mumbled in a low voice.

"Happy Birthday, Dad," Cliff answered through his tears.

Cliff sat, holding his dad's hand for what seemed like forever but was just a few minutes more, listening for those long pauses in the ragged breathing—until, at last, the pause arrived that never ended.

* * * *

"He's gorgeous, Sissy. A gorgeous baby boy. A Christmas baby," Susan's mother burbled with excitement as she lifted the bawling bundle from Sissy's arms to march over to the window into the corridor from where her husband could see his first grandchild for the first time.

Susan looked down at her bedraggled, but beaming, younger sister and squeezed her hand. Sissy squeezed back.

"There, now, that was worth it, wasn't it?" Susan asked. "And only about five hours longer than anyone could possibly have imagined."

Both sister's laughed and then Sissy grimaced from the pain of the exertion this required, but she smiled broadly again when Susan's face betrayed her concern.

"I don't know how I could have endured it without you being here, though," Sissy said to Susan. And then, "But wait. What *are* you doing here? You're supposed to be in Bermuda, aren't you?"

"We scotched that plan," Susan answered. "Some little birdie or other told me you were going to surprise us with a Christmas baby, and I wouldn't want to miss this for the world."

"What, you have second sight along with perfect skin and the world's sexiest husband?" the younger sister jabbed back at the older sister.

"Yes, something like that, I guess," Susan answered. But somehow she thought it was something much larger than that. She wouldn't question it; she'd just be mighty happy she and Cliff had been home for Christmas.

There was a tap on the window to the corridor and Susan looked up into the eyes of her husband who had just appeared there. One look into his eyes and she knew what he had to tell her. And, second sight, or not, Susan also knew that this Christmas at home had made their bond stronger than any second honeymoon cruise to Bermuda could have done.

Other Stories

Second Helping

"Oh, I'm sorry. Let me get you another tea."

"Harrumph. What I really could use is a second helping of the mashed potatoes. What I got looked like it was served up with a thimble—and the beans are stuck in them."

"Oh, that's OK, miss. That's OK, isn't it, Frank?" Margaret asked. She put a restraining hand on her husband's arm and looked up pleadingly at the waitress. "It's no bother. And, here, he can have my tea; I haven't touched mine yet." She took over the wiping up of the puddle of tea as the waitress went to get Frank another glass. "It was just an accident, Frank. Her arm was brushed by that man getting up from his table."

"I asked for peas. These are beans."

"Oh, Frank, beans are good for you. Peas are carbs. She looks so tired, the poor dear."

"Eh?"

"The waitress. She looks tired. And it's almost Christmas. I overheard the waitresses talking while we were looking at the menu. Ours has young two boys—and her husband's walked out on them. Isn't that sad, Frank? And she has to spend her Christmas here, working a shift—or so she said. She said her boys would be all alone Christmas morning. That they couldn't have their Christmas until after their friends had all had theirs. And then there wouldn't be much for them under the tree anyway."

Margaret looked at her husband, expecting some sort of response, but he was busy impounding beans from the mashed potatoes. She wondered if he'd turned his hearing aid off. And she was worried about the tip. First the spilled tea and then no peas, which wasn't the waitress's fault anyway—Margaret was sure the menu said beans. She'd overheard the waitresses talking, and she'd heard theirs had to make good tips tonight. And she knew Frank was stingy with that even when he wasn't upset with the service. She was surprised Frank didn't overhear them too. He was just as close to the service station as she was.

The waitress returned with another glass of iced tea for Frank. And she'd brought two small bowls as well, one with a scoop of mashed potatoes in it and one with peas.

"Here you go, hon," she said. "Sorry for the mix-up."

"Harrumph," Frank muttered.

Margaret's hand fluttered at the buttons of her sweater and she glanced around the room, wanting to know if anyone was watching them but not wanting to make eye contact if they were. She felt embarrassed. She was sure that the menu had said beans. And what Frank had already been served in mashed potatoes was more than she gave him at home. She wanted to say something about that, but she didn't want Frank making a scene here in public—well, more of a scene than he already had made. When she spoke next, it was a return to the Christmas the waitress faced.

"I heard our waitress say that whatever she got for her boys for Christmas had to come out of tonight's earnings—that she'd worked this extra shift and had to work Christmas morning just to have some money for their presents. Isn't that sad, Frank? Didn't you hear them saying that too?"

The only response was a sour look and another "harrumph," as Frank carefully mixed his peas in with his mashed potatoes.

"I mean it's Christmas," Margaret continued. "Maybe it would help if the boys had something really nice to open and play with Christmas morning. Maybe then it wouldn't bother them as much to be there alone."

Margaret was hoping that Frank would stop frowning and looking sour and would say something about the spirit of Christmas.

But when Frank answered, it was to complain about the peas. "These peas are mushy. It would have been better to bring me carrots. That man over there has candied carrots. They look better than these peas." He spent the rest of the meal glowering at his plate as if carrots would suddenly materialize. They didn't, though, and he eventually ate the peas and mashed potatoes. Margaret wasn't surprised; Frank liked peas better than he liked carrots.

At the end of the meal, after the bill had arrived, Frank fiddled around in his wallet and came up with the money to pay the tab on the way out, at the cash register by the door. As discretely as she could, Margaret took a five-dollar bill from her purse, and as Frank was struggling into his coat, she tucked the bill under her plate. Then she glanced around the edges of Frank's plate to see if he'd left anything at all.

She stood there at the table, stunned for a minute. "Um, Frank," she started to say.

"Get a move on there, woman," Frank answered in a grumbling voice. He had his hand on Margaret's arm, pulling her toward the cash register. "You'll miss your TV programs if we dawdle."

Margaret took one last look at the twenty-dollar bill Frank had left on the table before turning and putting her arm through Frank's and giving a little smile. He'd heard what she was saying about the waitress after all.

Second Glance

The contest notice had gone up at Thanksgiving time, and there'd been a little box on a back page of the local paper about it on the three subsequent Saturdays. It took no more than that for a mob of people, flying solo, teamed up in pairs, or organized into groups, to be swarming all over the Downtown Mall two evenings before Christmas.

Fred Turner stood outside the door into his jewelry store and rubbed his hands with glee, watching all the groups of searchers running from one end of the bricked pedestrian street to the other, lifting up garbage can lids and crouching down to peer into nooks and crannies. And two of the three television stations had already been here, panning on his store front and interviewing him. Even now he could see a truck from the third one pulling up to the barrier blocking the street that had crossed over beside his store when the pedestrian street had been the city's main street and had carried car traffic.

"Hot diggity dog," he thought. The original announcement had been made for free—again while he prominently stood in front of Turner's, his jewelry store. And the paper had even given him a cut rate on the Saturday advertisements and had done a front-page feature on him the previous weekend. Before Thanksgiving he'd been afraid that he'd have to close his doors, with the flashier jewelry store opening up on the Mall and folks increasingly doing their shopping on the Internet. But with all of the publicity this hunt had given him, his business was booming. And, he chuckled to himself, he was sure that, with his cleverness, he wouldn't even have to award the pearl necklace everyone was looking for.

He'd just been sitting watching television one night and the idea had, boom, just flashed into his brain. Madge had told him that it wasn't exactly a revelation and had probably come from one of the dozen reality hunt shows he was addicted to. But Madge was always a downer.

None of the hunt shows—that he was aware of—had come up with the kicker he had to have the hunt but not to have much risk of losing the prize.

The rules were pretty simple. There was a first-class pearl necklace, worth nearly a thousand dollars, to be had by anyone who found it in its, as he put it in the advertisements, "precious vessel" between the hours of two and four in the afternoon, today. The hunters were assured that it could be found within sight of the Downtown Mall. And all they had to do to register was buy a twenty-dollar gift certificate redeemable at Turner's before the end of January. In exchange they got a red baseball cap with Turner's Jewelry arcing over the brim. (That had been Madge's idea.) All they had to do to win was to find the necklace and be wearing one of the Turner's red baseball caps when they came back to the store. And they had to agree to be filmed shaking hands with Fred Turner to be covered by the media.

Fred was in seventh heaven standing outside his door and watching a sea of red baseball hats with his logo on them bobbing all around the Mall. He laughed at seeing where people were thinking of looking. One guy was up in a tree, tangled in the fairy lights, and checking out the crooks of the branches. A woman was using a limb trimmer she'd brought with her to fiddle around behind the marquee of the movie theater that had been morphed into a stage theater to see if she could bring a "precious vessel" down from there. A group of teenagers were stumbling over the legs of a panhandler outside of the door of the pawn shop across the way from Fred as they checked through the sale items that had been put out on a bookshelf that the bum was huddled against for warmth.

One of the teenagers actually went down, tripping over the legs of the unseen bum, but instead of getting up or saying anything at all to the panhandler, he took advantage of his newly acquired ground-level perspective to search under a planter that was marking off what would be an outside café area when warmer weather came.

And, speaking of warmer weather, Fred realized that it had begun to snow. He took one more self-satisfied look around the pedestrian mall, seeing that eyes were darting around everywhere, assessing where a "precious vessel" big enough to hold a pearl necklace would be seen. They were looking everywhere except at the panhandler. Nobody was looking at the panhandler. It was as if he didn't exist.

Fred mused on that for a moment. The same panhandler was out there nearly every day, rain or shine—or snow, like today. And yet no one really saw him. That was strange, Fred thought, but maybe not that strange. People don't look at what they don't want to see, what they don't want to believe exists, even in a wealthy little city in the United States.

But it was getting too cold for Fred to philosophize out on the sidewalk. And it was getting dark and pushing on toward four. The pace of the hunt out on the Mall was getting frenzied, but the crowd was thinning out. People weren't leaving, though. They weren't giving up. They wouldn't give up until four. But some of the more venturesome ones were expanding their search, moving outside of the Mall, checking possible hiding places that weren't actually on the Mall but were within sight of it.

Fred wasn't worried. If they hadn't found it right away, he didn't think they'd ever find it.

As he entered the store, he turned to close the door on the chill in the air and saw, through the falling snowflakes, that the panhandler had struggled to a standing position and was moving his way.

Instinctively, Fred retreated back to behind his counter, putting a barrier between himself and the outside world and drifting into the shadows of the store's interior. Perhaps the bum would only come up to the window. Surely he wouldn't come inside.

But maybe he did intend to come inside, Fred thought. He couldn't have that. So, he came back from behind the counter and marched toward the door.

Before either he or the panhandler got to the store door, however, the panhandler was intercepted by a ragtag woman all bundled up in many layers of clothes—all the clothes she owned, Fred thought with a sniff of his nose. He assessed her as just one of the bag ladies who frequented the Mall and had helped ruin his business before he'd come up with this hunt idea. She was wearing one of the red baseball hats he'd issued for the hunt, and, with a flash of anger, Fred wondered where in the heck she'd gotten that.

"You look cold," he heard the woman say to the panhandler. "You can come over to First Church with me, if you like. It's only two blocks. They're serving a free dinner this evening. They open their doors at four, though, so we can get warm."

"I don't know . . ." The panhandler's teeth were chattering so hard from the cold that he struggled to get even that much of a sentence out. "But maybe I can. It's after four now, isn't it?"

"Oh, and you don't even have gloves. It's too cold for that," the woman said, not commenting on the time. For people like her and this young man, there was little need to think of time. "And it's snowing," she continued. "Here, I have several pairs. Let me hold that . . . what is it? Some sort of wooden baby's cradle? . . . long enough for you to slip these gloves on."

Fred Turner stood there, aghast, as the bag lady took up the wooden cradle from the store's crèche that he had paid a pittance to the panhandler to hold between the hours of two and four today, and, as she took it into her arms, espied the gleaming pearl necklace nestled in the white cotton wadding stuffed inside the manger replica Fred had chosen to hold the necklace as his own little "precious vessel" joke. He looked up at the clock on his wall. It was 3:55.

Second Christmas

"Look at this present, Laura. What do you think is in it? I had to go to three stores, and it cost a bundle, I can tell you."

"Open mine next, if you please, Laura. That one over there with the iPod in it. Oh, damn, you didn't hear me say that, did you? She didn't hear me say that, did she? I have a conference call in ten minutes, so I'll have to go to the library."

"Don't you just love that, Laura? A gift card to the Charlotte Russe store from your grandmother and grandfather. We'll have to telephone them your thanks, won't we? When they get back from their cruise."

"If we're going to have everything else ready when the turkey's done, I'll need to go out to the kitchen and light a fire under Florence. Maybe you'd like to come with me, May. You're so talented at finishing off a table."

There was a flurry of movement as the room cleared toward exits to other rooms, and for the next few minutes it was only Laura and Uncle Harry in the living room next to the eight-foot real Scotch pine that was glowing so brightly that no other light was needed in the room. Well, she'd been told to call him Uncle Harry. He was Gerald's brother, not really much of a relation to Laura. Gerald, who Laura was working hard to think of calling Dad, was Laura's mother's new husband—the second one since Laura's own father.

Laura hadn't even half finished opening all of her presents yet, and the only one left in the room to watch her was Uncle Harry—and he looked like he wanted to be somewhere else himself. Any place else, really. And after the downing of his drink, a few huffs, a couple of starts on "Well . . . ," and a relighting of his pipe with fumbling hands, he mumbled something about needing to be somewhere. And then Uncle Harry was gone too.

Just a few minutes before, the room had been full of people—Laura's mother and stepfather, Aunt May and Uncle Harry, and even Florence, standing at the door into the dining room and drying her hands on an apron and beaming at Laura, the dazzle of the lights reflected in her kindly face.

But that had lasted for maybe about fifteen minutes, as Laura's mother pushed wrapped present after present off on her from under the gigantic tree until Laura was afraid she would be buried under them. Laura hardly had time to open one before there would be another one in her lap, accompanied by the insistence to open that next and to be ever so grateful that all of this money was being spent on her for things that were either too young or too old for her—or so delicate and precious that they'd have to be put behind glass forever. Laura's mother was that kind of woman. Laura was surprised that she didn't have a dance lesson and swim team meet to go to before noon as well—with her mother running off to do some shopping while Laura added to her future college admissions portfolio.

Only Florence's present, a pretty crystal necklace, was something that Laura had mentioned wanting. But then Florence was the only one around the house enough—and listening to Laura enough—to have any idea what Laura liked.

At Thanksgiving Laura's grandmother—the mother of her mother—had gushed about how lovely it would be for the whole family to be together at Christmas, and so Laura's mother had dutifully gotten her husband to postpone their own trip out to Las Vegas that week. Grandmother Wren really liked the new husband of Laura's mother. He had an important job in the city that had him—and often Laura's mother with him—flying all over the country. And he belonged to that country club where

Grandfather Wren liked to golf every day. But a good deal on a Caribbean cruise had come up, so Laura's grandparents weren't here today. They had, however, given Laura a gift card for the trendy teenage clothing shop, Charlotte Russe—which would have been wonderful if Charlotte Russe made clothes for an eleven year old. Laura wondered how long these gift cards were good for.

What Laura remembered most about Thanksgiving was how Grandmother Wren kept going on and on about the jeans Laura was wearing and saying how young women in her day wore skirts and blouses and looked like proper young ladies. Laura supposed that was what the gift card for the Charlotte Russe store was all about.

Laura—all alone in the living room—was still opening presents and trying to keep the tags with them when the Christmas dinner started in the dining room. She could hear the clinking of glasses and the boisterous voices from where she was, but her mother had told her as they were coming downstairs to "discover what Santa brought" that all of the presents had to be opened before Laura's dad picked her up for her second Christmas at his apartment. So Laura had concentrated on that task.

"My land, child, you're still here."

Laura looked up to see Florence standing in the doorway to the dining room with a gravy boat cradled in her hands.

"I saw that your chair was empty, but your mother said she thought your father had already picked you up."

"No, he hasn't come yet," Laura answered. "He wanted me to be at his place for dinner, but mother told him no."

Florence's lips pursed, and she was about to say something, but Laura rushed on. "Thank you for the necklace, Florence. It's really, really nice. Just what I wanted."

"Well, best you keep it somewhere other than your jewelry box, young lady. I know for a fact that your mother looks in there regularly. When I mentioned your wantin' that to your mother, she said that crystals were too common to be worn. And right now, why don't you come into the kitchen and eat with me? The others are about done and they're already talkin' about scatterin' with the wind."

"Thanks, Florence. The necklace is really, really . . ." Laura started to repeat. But just then the doorbell rang and when Florence and Laura met at the door, they saw that it was Laura's father, Bill, standing out there and moving from one foot to the other in an attempt to stay warm in his thin jacket against the snowfall from the previous night.

"Hello, Princess. Sorry I'm early, but I couldn't wait to see you on Christmas morning. Oh, what a pretty necklace. Are you going to wear that over to my place?"

Bill Treadwell's apartment was dimly lit and scruffy in contrast to the home of Laura's new stepfather on the sixth hole of the country club. It wasn't just that the wattage of the bulbs in the two squat, mismatched table lamps was inadequate to the task but also because there were no lights on the Christmas tree, a sickly looking aluminum table-top tree perched on the dining table at one end of the living-dining room combination.

This tree was the first thing that lit up Laura's eyes when she entered the apartment.

"Daddy, isn't that—?"

"Yes, Princess. It's the tree we bought at that yard sale when you were five—the one we were going to put in your bedroom."

"Didn't Mom . . .?"

"I pulled it out of the garbage and kept it. I thought you'd like to have it for Christmas again. Sorry that it's bent. I think it was that way when we bought it, though—but you wanted it. And, look, those ornaments you made at school . . ."

"Oh, Daddy. I . . ."

Laura didn't get any farther, because that's when she made her second discovery. "Grams, Pops, you came," she squealed. And then she launched herself at the couch and landed between her grandmother and grandfather Treadwell, where she was swallowed up in arms, soft padding, and hugs.

"I know your dad told you we couldn't be here this Christmas, sweetie," Laura's grandmother said. "But I can have a toe operation anytime. I just rescheduled it."

Laura looked around the room then and noticed that the small space was stuffed with people sitting around on mismatched dining room chairs and cheerily talking. In addition to her dad and grandparents, there was Aunt Jessica, her dad's sister, and her husband and their toddler, and then two others, an elderly man and a tiny woman, both of whom her dad introduced as neighbors in the apartment house who hadn't had other plans for Christmas.

All of them—except the toddler, who really wanted to swing on the drapes in the living room window but who was good-naturedly pulled down and swung around the room like he was an airplane—zeroed in on Laura and wanted to know all of the things she'd gotten in her first Christmas of the day.

Laura talked about the gifts she could remember among all that she'd gotten at her stepfather's house, not even all opened yet, while plates of food were passed around—all pot luck from those who were there that day.

"I always wanted a crystal necklace but never got one," her Aunt Jessica told her, as she pulled the toddler off the drapes again. From the expression on his face, Laura knew that her little cousin only went for the drapes to get the plane ride.

While she was talking about her presents, glowing more because everyone seemed genuinely to be more interested in talking with her than in the presents themselves, Laura looked over at the tree and saw that there were no presents under its silvery branches—just the cardboard crèche and plaster figurines her dad had collected when he was her age. No matter, though, she thought. She knew her dad was stretched to make ends meet. Having saved that old aluminum tree and put it up for her was present enough—she had more presents back at her stepfather's house than she could even remember. She'd still be unwrapping them and trying to remember who to write the thank-you note to tomorrow.

That's when her father entered from the kitchen, bundling a squirming something in his arms, and all eyes, including Laura's went to him.

"Daddy!" she cried out. "A kitten."

"Yes, Princess. And she's all yours. Merry Christmas, sweetheart."

"But . . ."

"I know. Your mother told you you couldn't have one. And she's right, the kitten would scratch up her furniture and leave cat hair everywhere. But we'll keep it here. Not much harm it can do here. It can be our secret. You can visit it whenever you come."

Laura took the kitten from his arms and was mostly lost to whatever was happening in the apartment after that.

A couple of hours later, when all of the other guests were gone and Laura's dad was getting ready to drive her back to the house on the sixth hole of the country club golf course, he knelt down beside her and the kitten.

"I hope you had a good Christmas, Princess. I know we couldn't provide all of the presents and pretty tree for the second Christmas that I saw when I came to pick up you. I just hope . . ."

"Daddy?"

"Yes, sweetheart?"

"I loved the second Christmas. Can I . . . can I stay here tonight. Just for tonight . . . and sleep with the kitten? The couch would be fine."

"Sure, honey," Bill murmured through the tears forming in his eyes. "I already talked to your mother. She didn't think you'd want to stay, but she said it was OK if you did—that she and her husband would be out late at his office Christmas party anyway."

Seconds

"You don' mind that it came from Clarence and don' fit too well yet?"

"Naw, it's fine, Mom. Look it's got pockets below as well as above. Regular huntin' shorts. And I can jus' cinch the belt real tight for a while."

"They come to below your knees. I don' think . . . maybe I should tell Angelic 'no thanks.'"

"They'll be OK, Mom."

"I did so want to outfit you new for the spring term."

But Terrence didn't hear me say this. He was already jumping up and running out of the apartment to go show Larry his new hunter shorts. Well, not new. Seconds. Hand-me-downs. Again. That seemed to be the way our life went. Living on seconds. Even when we went shopping for new clothes, they were no newer than whatever the Goodwill store had.

But Terrence was always so nice about it. He didn't seem to mind. That bothered me more than anything else. He should mind. At least I think he should. He's better than that. My son isn't a second; he's a first.

But no use going into that. I sighed and looked at the clock. I was pushing toward late getting to the Jackson's house. They needed the extra help setting up for Christmas. They were having a big Christmas Eve bash, and they were the kind who had a decorated tree in every room and who changed over all of their other things for the season.

The Jacksons were nice folks, though. Terrence had gotten a lot of nice hand-me-downs from their son, Scott. And lord knows I could use the extra money in this season. I'd have to find extra hours to work for Terrence and me even to have one scrawny tree.

When I entered the Jackson's house, they were in full battle in struggling to get the decorations out. Mrs. Jackson sent me to the garage for a hammer, where I found Mr. Jackson sawing away at branches of a Scotch pine to give it a perfect shape. The Jackson's were big on perfect shapes.

"When you need a break, Celia, come and get me," he said as I was rummaging around where Mrs. Jackson said the hammers were, but not finding one. He came over with a smile on his face and pulled a hammer out for me. "There's something down in the basement I'd like you to see."

I'd worked for a couple of hours without a break, though, and he came for me.

"You need a break, Celia," he said. "Get a soft drink out of the fridge and then come down to the basement."

I did as he asked, grateful that he'd come for me. I did need a break, but there was so much to do, and Mrs. Jackson was buzzing around in high gear herself. I didn't want her to think I was being lazy on her.

"What do you think?" he asked when we'd descended the basement stairs and he flipped on the lights.

"That's a mighty something special," I replied. And it was. Laid out on a Ping-Pong table in the center of the room was what looked like a whole village, with a road running like a snake all around it. Looking through all of the houses and trees and other stuff jazzing up the scene, I could see that it was some sort of fancy race car track with all of the jags and turns and obstacles. There was a big, humming transformer sitting in one corner of the table, which was probably what was lighting up all the houses and would make the cars race too. "It's really something special," I repeated.

"Do you think Terrence might like to have it?" he asked.

"Excuse me, Mr. J.?" I sputtered. "Terrence have somethin' like this?"

"It was Scott's. He's outgrown it, and we thought that you might like to have it for Terrence for Christmas."

I didn't know what to think. But, that wasn't true. I did know what to think. But if I'd said the first thing I thought, it would be ungrateful. And the Jacksons had been real good to me—and to Terrence too. And normally it would be a wonderful thing for them to do for Terrence. It looked like it was in almost new condition. I was sure they could have sold it. And for a pretty penny too. But there was something else in my mind. And it wasn't all pride—or the dejection I'd been feeling the past couple of months about Terrence and seconds.

"Uh, thanks, Mr. J. But Terrence isn't really into such things. It's such a nice set that I wouldn't want it to go unused."

It sounded lame to me, but Mr. Jackson seemed to accept it at face value, and with just an "Oh, well, it was just an idea" and a "no, it shouldn't go unused. Scott enjoyed it so much," we were clumping back upstairs to resume the house beautiful Christmas makeover.

Mrs. Jackson went over the menu for the Christmas Eve party with me before I left and, I'm happy to say, told me they'd pay me triple time for working on Christmas Eve.

Their party went off perfectly. With the Jacksons you could count on that.

Late Christmas morning I was surprised to hear the door chime as I was fixing lunch.

Mr. and Mrs. Jackson were at the door, all smiles, and holding a Christmas basket.

I could see that most of the things that were in it were leftovers from their party the previous evening. Still, it was awfully nice of them to come out on Christmas day to bring me—and, I'm sure, others—Christmas baskets. And it was mighty good food they'd laid out the previous evening.

I didn't even think of it as seconds. Well, I did, I guess. But I certainly didn't resent it. The Jacksons were good people. And they were showing the right Christmas spirit, if you ask me. Besides, seconds were good enough for me.

I didn't ask them in, saying that we were about to sit down for lunch, and they didn't seem to mind, saying they had several other stops to make.

I felt bad about not asking them in, but I think my reason was good—even for them, who had shown such a generous, well-meaning spirit.

When they were walking down the apartment hall stairs and I closed the door, I turned to watch Terrence finishing up putting together the track for that small race car set I'd bought for him at Wal-Mart—that I'd bought new a week before Mr. Jackson offered me Scott's fancy set.

I would have been mortified for Mr. Jackson to see that Terrence obviously was delighted with the race car set, even if it didn't run on electricity—as he was showing by being completely glorified in putting his new one together. His new one. I'm sure that, if I explained it, the Jacksons would understand. But they were too nice for me to want to explain it to them. It was just that this once, just this once, I wanted my son to be the first in having something, even if it wasn't much.

To me, my son wasn't a second; he was a first.

Second Job

Joyce had barely made it back to the apartment from the grocery store where she worked as a checkout clerk and tucked away the ham she'd brought home—the last one in the store—before it was time to go pick up the Christmas cake she'd ordered from Gleesons before they closed. She had already been cutting her time short—she still had to go buy a tree and figure out where she'd stashed the ornaments and lights—and she hadn't gotten off shift when she expected to. She kicked herself for not remembering that Christmas Eve could be a mad house in the grocery store, particularly since they closed at 8:00 PM that night even though they usually stayed open around the clock.

She could have left on time, but they were shorthanded and the other clerks looked so frazzled with the last-minute rush that she'd decided to stay an extra fifteen minutes and help them out. The next time she had looked up it was an hour later.

Now she was as frazzled as any of the other clerks and running terribly behind on setting up for Christmas. Christina would be getting in from her college late tonight, and Joyce wanted her otherwise dreary apartment to be all aglow with Christmas for her daughter.

She had jammed the ham in the refrigerator and was heading for the door when her cell phone buzzed. Joyce looked at the caller ID. It was Mrs. Franklin. No way she couldn't take this call.

Mrs. Franklin was one of Joyce's regulars from her other job—her second job. The job that provided the money that Joyce lived on. The money from her regular, full-time job all went to keeping Christina in college.

"Hello, Mrs. Franklin," she said, as she exited the apartment and started down the two flights of stairs to the parking lot. "And a Merry Christmas to you."

"I don't know what I'll do, Joyce. I managed to pull the tree out of the attic, but I can't get it down the stairs—and I have no idea at all how to set it up. I told George just to put a plastic bag over it after last year, not to break it down. But there it is all boxed back up, and it's Christmas Eve, and I don't know how . . ."

"Hang on and don't try to pull it down the stairs yourself, Mrs. Franklin. I'll be right over."

It was this second job that was going to kill Joyce, she always thought. But then, each time she thought that, she bit her tongue. It was the second job—the people she helped—that had kept her going ever since Christina went off to college and, without knowing it, ripped that big hole in Joyce's life. Joyce couldn't any more let Mrs. Franklin drag a tree down to her living room and try to figure out how to put it together than she was able to say "You should have done this weeks ago" to Mrs. Devan earlier this afternoon when Joyce was going to make cookies but had been called out instead to take Mrs. Devan to do her Christmas shopping. Mrs. Franklin's life had been a fluttering "I didn't know that had to be done" ever since her George had died back in the spring.

So the cookies weren't made. Joyce had brought some home from the grocery store that were at least store made, although she knew Christina wouldn't be fooled into thinking they were homemade.

This happened to Joyce a lot since she'd taken on this second job. The service was called Helping Hand, and the people who worked for it had a list of clients—mostly the old and the infirm—who could, and did, call on them night and day to help with whatever they needed doing, from opening a tight-lidded jelly jar to wading around in a flooded basement looking for a water cutoff.

Joyce had thought it was a nifty idea and a needed service—and she still thought that. And she thought it was very nice that, on an hourly basis, it paid better than her grocery store clerk job. She had found, however, that, on the whole, it was more demanding and challenging than the grocery store job. It also, though, was more personally rewarding.

Mrs. Franklin didn't only want the tree put together; she needed someone—Joyce being that someone—to put the lights and ornaments on it and to do some more decorating of the living room as well.

It was while Joyce was finishing this up that she got the call from old Mr. Strang.

"I need you over here right now. It's an emergency."

Mr. Strang was never the one to waste words.

"What is it? What do you need done, Mr. S.?" Joyce asked.

"Can't say over the phone. But it's an emergency."

Everything was an emergency with Mr. Strang, but Joyce remembered that one time when he'd been this abrupt and unhelpful Joyce had arrived to find him stuck in the bathtub— there for two days before thinking of using the telephone his daughter had had installed right beside the tub. He hadn't put it there, he said. So why should he have to remember that someone else had?

"Don't bother to take off your coat. You have to take me out. It's an emergency." Mr. Strang was standing just inside his door, all bundled up, when Joyce arrived.

"What is it? Are you not feeling well? Palpitations? A tightness in your chest?" Mr. Strang was prone to believing he had any disease he heard of. But as far as Joyce could tell he was as healthy as a man twenty-five years younger. But, then, a sixty-year-old man could have a good reason to suddenly need to go to the emergency room.

"Need a ham. A pretty big one."

"You need a ham?"

"Yep. In case you haven't noticed, it's Christmas Eve."

"Yes, I'm aware of that, Mr. S. And being as how it's Christmas Eve—9:00 o'clock Christmas Eve now—I'm afraid we aren't going to find a grocery store open."

"How do ya know that?" Mr. Strang was giving Joyce a highly suspicious look. "Maybe you just don't want to make the effort to help me find a Christmas ham."

As well as being a slight hypochondriac, Mr. Strang was not particularly trusting or diplomatic. Joyce had broken through his cantankerous shell a long time ago, though, and found a fascinating man who had been both a rake and an adventurer in his youth.

"I'm a grocery clerk in my other life, Mr. S. You know that. I think that qualifies me for knowing what grocery stores carrying hams will be open at 9:00 o'clock on Christmas Eve. None of them, I'm afraid. I got the last ham at our store this evening myself, as a matter of fact."

He wasn't taking off his coat. He was just standing there, looking at Joyce expectantly.

This wasn't the greatest time for him to suddenly put his full trust in her, she thought. And then she also thought about what she'd just told him—that she'd bought the last ham her store had that very evening.

"Take your coat off and go back to your easy chair, Mr. S. I know where I can get a ham. I'll go get it and bring it to you."

Joyce was almost all the way back to Mr. Strang's apartment, with her ham sitting on the car seat next to her, when her cell phone buzzed again. Joyce had a sudden impulse to roll the car window down and toss the phone out. It was Ms. Barden, her old elementary school teacher, who had found out that Joyce had gone to work for Helping Hands and then had insisted that her former student be assigned to her account.

Ms. Barden was a sweety, but she never had been able to keep track of where her eyeglasses were or to be fully prepared for much of anything.

This evening was no exception.

112

"I have to have a cake baked in an hour for a party, and I find I don't have everything I need. Can you help?"

"Sure, Ms. Barden," Joyce said with a sigh. The sigh wasn't really for Eve Barden. It was in remembrance that Joyce hadn't made it to Gleesons before closing to pick up that special cake she had told Christina she'd ordered. It had once been a tradition in their family—when they had been a happy family. Every Christmas Eve they'd get Christina whatever special cake Gleesons was making that year.

They hadn't done that for years, not since Eddie died, really. But Christina had mentioned it when she'd called about plans on getting home for Christmas, and Joyce had said they'd do that again. So she'd decided to splurge and ordered a special Gleesons Christmas cake. The cakes were so popular that people who hadn't made their order in time stood around at closing time, hoping that someone wouldn't pick up their cake. Some other family was probably already eating Christina's cake.

Joyce felt like crying, but she pulled herself together. She had a job to do. These old folks depended on her and she wouldn't let them down. It was too late not to let Christina down. And it wasn't just the cake. It was after nine, and Joyce didn't even have a tree yet.

Well, she'd see about a tree on the way home to get whatever Ms. Barden needed for her cake.

"What do you need, Ms. Barden? I'll bring it to you if I can find it at home."

"Flour and sugar mainly. And maybe a few eggs. Oh, and do you happen to have any vanilla?"

"I think I can rustle that up," Joyce answered with a little sigh.

"Oh, and I suppose it should have some icing. Maybe you have whatever goes into that."

"Yes, of course, Ms. Barden. I'll be right over."

"You might bring a recipe book too. I'm a little rusty at this. In fact, I'm not sure I've ever made a cake."

Joyce stopped at three tree lots—three mostly empty Christmas tree lots—on her way home to get the ingredients and a recipe book for Ms. Barden's Christmas cake.

And when she got home with a scrawny little tree with bare branches on one side she was fuming at herself for not having bought something at the first stand and then having run out of time. Christina would be home about midnight, and there was barely time to get to Ms. Barden's, make the cake, and then drive Ms. Barden to her party. The woman had dropped the fact that the party wasn't at her house, and Ms. Barden didn't drive.

It was 11:15 when Joyce got Ms. Barden and her Christmas cake to her party, which turned out to be at Mrs. Franklin's house.

"Here you are, Ms. Barden. Hope you have a great party."

"Could you carry the cake in for me, dear? I'm so afraid I'll drop it."

"More likely you'll forget to take it," was what Joyce was thinking. But she was so resigned to having completely failed to get Christmas set up for Christina—having remembered when she thought back on taking Mrs. Devan Christmas shopping that afternoon that she'd forgotten to buy the gift for Christina she'd thought so long and hard on getting—that she merely smiled and opened her car door. "Sure thing, Mrs. Barden. You go on up to the door, and I'll bring in the cake."

When Joyce reached the door, so preoccupied was she with searching her mind on what she'd do with the tree in the fifteen minutes she'd probably have between getting home and Christina arriving, that the three-part harmony "Surprise!" that rang out from inside Mrs. Franklin's living room didn't register at first.

What registered first was wondering what Christina was doing in Mrs. Franklin's parlor, her smile lighting up the room and holding one of the Gleesons special Christmas cakes. Joyce's eyes then swept the room, picking out Mrs. Franklin standing in the light of the tree that they'd both decorated earlier that evening; Mr. Strang, holding his—no, her—ham on a platter;

Mrs. Devan, with an armful of wrapped presents; and even a couple of her checkout clerk girlfriends from the grocery store.

Christina spoke into the void that Joyce, throat choked with emotion, couldn't fill with her own voice.

"I hope you don't mind, Mom. Your friends here contacted me and told me what a help you'd been to them all year and that they wanted to do something special for you on Christmas Eve. I told them I couldn't be happier than to share our Christmas with your larger family."

The Author

Olivia Stowe is a published author under different names and in other dimensions of fiction and nonfiction and lives quietly in a university town with an indulgent spouse.

Olivia is proudly published by

www.cyberworldpublishing.com